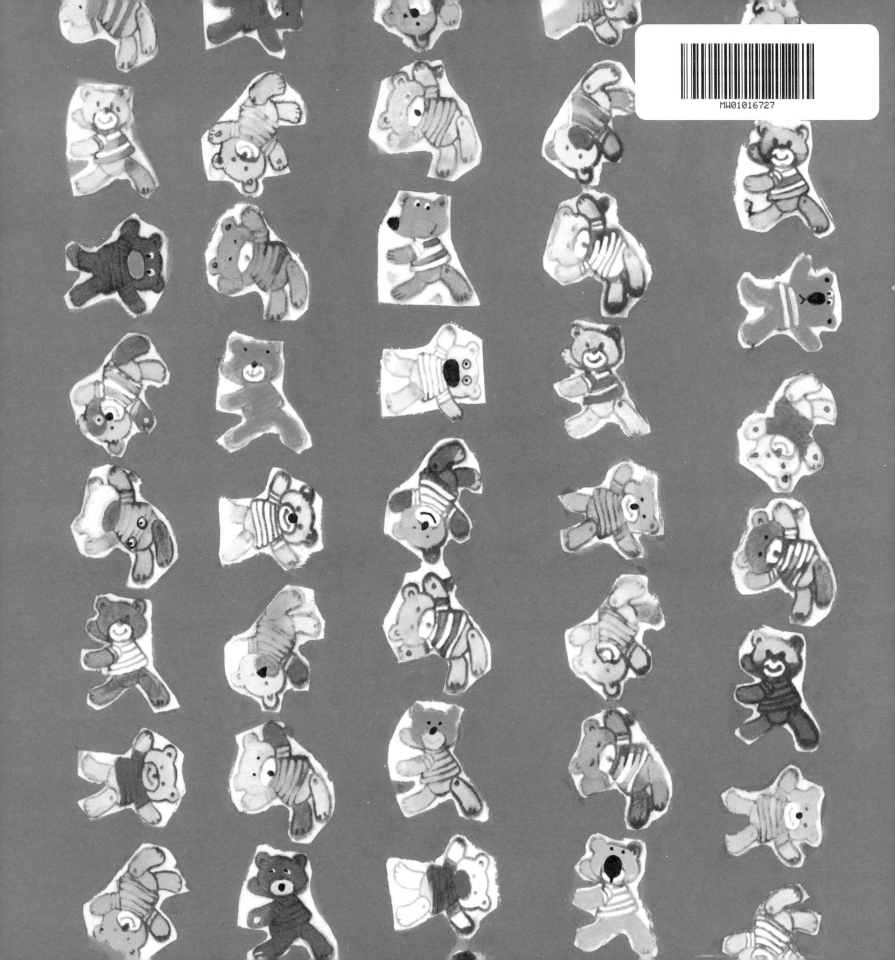

Apolline and her Bear

Published by Céthial Books for Children
An Imprint of Céthial&Bossche Pro. Inc.
300 Saint Sacrement Suite 307
Montreal, Que. H2Y 1X4

Copyright © 2000 Céthial&Bossche Pro. Inc.

First Edition
10 9 8 7 6 5 4 3 2 1
ISBN: 1-894155-00-9
Library of Congress Catalog Card Number:
National Library of Canada

Distributed by Céthial&Bossche Consumer Products

Phone: 1-888-265-2479
Email: cethial@cethial.com
Céthial On Line: www.cethial.com

Apolline and Her Bear

Nadine Walter

Illustrations by Robert Scouvart

Apolline had gone to bed early. Her dance class that day at the Young Dancers Academy in Paris had been long and hard.

"Heels, toes! Heels, toes! Keep in time, young ladies! Keep in time!" The dance teacher had made them practice and practice and practice.

Now Apolline was delighted to snuggle up in bed under her down comforter.

The headlights of cars passing by on the street cast strange shadows on her bedroom walls.

Apolline's eyelids grew heavier and heavier. Peace and quiet surrounded her.

Little did she know a whirlwind was about to descend on her little world!

ater that night, much later, there came a loud knock at her door.
At first she thought it was someone trying to come into her dream,
a fantastic story filled with puppets, clowns, and blind mice.

It wasn't a dream. There really was someone outside the door!

Knock . . . knock . . . knock. . .

Apolline propped herself up on her elbow
and looked anxiously at her closed door.

Who had come to see her so late at night? "C-come in," she said, heart
thumping. The door opened slowly. "Oh, my!" said Apolline, gaping.

There stood a big bear, right in her doorway!
His eyes were as round as brown marbles and his snout
was twitching as though he had found a jar of honey.

Then the bear came into her room, closed the door,
and, with his front paw, switched on the light.

The bear was plump and furry! "Where did you come from?" asked
Apolline. "What are you doing in my room?" The bear paid no attention to
her questions and walked right past her. Suddenly everything
looked tiny as the bear's huge body seemed to fill the room.
He looked around, then headed for the toy box. When he opened it,
the china doll perched on top tumbled to the floor.

Apolline was bursting with curiosity. "What are you
looking for, Bear?"

His behavior was rather odd. He dumped all her toys out
of the box, but he didn't play with any of them! When
everything lay in a mess around him, the bear stood up.

"Grrr! Grrr!" he growled.

Apolline's heart beat wildly. She wondered what he
would do next. Suddenly, the strange visitor crossed the
room, turned off the light, and left the bedroom.
"Gee," murmured the little girl. "What a funny visit!
I wonder what he wanted?"

In the morning, Apolline's mother stood in the doorway, shocked.
"Your bedroom looks like a hurricane struck it. Everything is topsy-turvy!"
"It wasn't a hurricane, it was a bear as big as this," said Apolline excitedly.
She told her mother the whole story of the bear's
strange night visit. Alas, her mother didn't believe a word of it.
"You were dreaming, my dear. Now you'll just have to put everything
back in its place and clean your room."

8

hat night, Apolline was on pins and needles. Would her strange visitor return? Sure enough, late that night, slowly, very slowly, the door opened. It was the bear! "Good evening, Bear!" she greeted him, but he ignored her, just like the night before. With his clumsy, heavy gait, he headed toward her closet, opened it up wide, and sent all of her clothes flying. Wham! Zing! Sweaters, shirts, socks, T-shirts–it all came out. Bang! Wham!

"Darn it," said Apolline, frowning.
"Is that all you know how to do? Make a mess?"

Then she had an idea. "Wait a minute! I know–you want to play hot-or-cold, isn't that so?"

Ignoring her, the bear went over to the curtains and shook them. Apolline, her eyes bright with excitement, bounced to her feet. "Over here?"

The bear paid no attention to her and took a box off the shelf. "Is that it, are you getting hotter?" asked Apolline.

Hardly had he opened the box, full of lovely pearl shells she had found at the seashore, than he pushed it away. "Grrr! Grrr!" Apolline nodded her head. "Well, I guess it's not there. Cold, cold, cold!"

For an instant the bear paused. Then, suddenly he headed toward a chair piled high with various things. He grunted happily. His eyes were bright and shiny. Apolline held her breath. Was this it at last? "Red hot this time?"

"Me oh my, on fire! Quick, call the fire department!"

She laughed and jumped for joy, but shucks, triple shucks, the bear didn't seem to be celebrating. He frowned. "Grrr! Grrr!"

Disappointed, Apolline sighed heavily. "Poor old bear! Maybe you're headed for the North Pole. After all, maybe that's what you're looking for, an iceberg?"

The bear sniffed, lumbered across the room, turned off the light, and left, just like the night before!

Once again, Apolline found herself stuck with a big mess. Once more, she had to pick things up, fold clothes, and put stuff away. It wasn't fun, but she didn't moan and groan about it. Better to get the job done before mother noticed the disaster. She might get upset!

All next day, Apolline thought about the bear; she could hardly wait for bedtime. Under the covers she slipped, her eyes wide open and glued to the clock, but the bear was late. "Oh, I hope you come back," she sighed, "I miss you, Bear!"

The moment she heard his steps approaching her door, she jumped out of bed and greeted him with a smile.

"Good evening, Bear. Listen, I've given it a lot of thought and I know you're looking for something special. So I'm going to help you. Together we'll find it more easily, don't you think?" The bear growled a few times.

Definitely still grumpy! This time he went toward the desk. Apolline hoped he would respond, but . . . nothing. It was last night all over again. He threw books, pads of paper, her pencil sharpener, felt-tip markers, notebooks, erasers, and paints over his shoulder.

Bam! Smack! Thud! Zing!

Apolline looked at him with her little hands clenched in anger. "I've had enough of picking up my room by myself every night!" she said.

Still she loved the bear dearly. He certainly was a strange one, but everyone knows bears are short on manners. "The problem is that he messes things up, and messes them up again! Maybe it's a bear game. Well, I'll enjoy myself too," decided Apolline.

And she joined in with the bear. It was such fun to throw her notebooks! And her homework and pencils, wood blocks and dolls! Things flew hither and thither, they swirled, bounced off the bed, got tangled up in the sheets, rolled on the floor.

"Ha, ha, ha. This is so much fun, Bear! So much fun!" Toys and books whirled in the air like snowflakes falling crazily from the sky. Apolline laughed merrily. "You're right, Bear, it's great fun to make a mess!" But the bear wasn't laughing with her. On the contrary! He looked furious, and moved away from the little girl.

"Well, that does it!" said Apolline, flushed with anger, her hands on her hips. "You don't want me to help you and you don't even want me to play with you. So why do you come to my room every night?" As usual, the bear ignored her. Like before, he turned off the light and left the bedroom.

"This doesn't make any sense!" said Apolline as she sank down on her bed. "This is one mysterious bear. He comes and makes a mess and then-poof!-he disappears! And I can't even talk to Mother about it."

So, on the fourth night, Apolline decided to stay in bed. She'd had enough of those silly bear games. As always, the bear knocked, came in, and switched on the light, but this time something had changed. He seemed to have a bear smile on his furry face.

Before Apolline could say a word, the bear rushed across the room and grabbed a small cloth bag with a pair of pink ballet slippers sticking out. It was her dance bag.

The bear took the ballet slippers and held them to his heart, snorting happily. "Aha!" said Apolline. "So that's what you were looking for? My ballet slippers?" The bear nodded his head vigorously. An answer at last. "And you chose my bedroom because I'm a dancer?"

He nodded again, as he tried to put on the ballet slippers. Of course, they were much too small, but he pushed his paws into them anyway. The bear had a dream, and that dream was to be a dancer, which might seem strange, because everyone knows bears aren't born to dance.

Then he leaped up and sprang across the room, attempting a very difficult leap, knocking over the chair and desk in the process. The poor thing was so clumsy!

"My dear Bear, you're completely ridiculous," said Apolline kindly. Yes, he was clumsy to be sure, but so very funny as a prima ballerina! The bear leaped, bounded, slid, and twirled as clumsily as a bull in a china shop. He was so comical that Apolline couldn't help laughing, but she also felt a surge of affection for him.

Standing on her tiptoes, she encouraged him with hints. "Look, Bear, do like I do: heel, toe: heel, toe, and up and up! Yippee! Now round your arms like an arch over your head. Wonderful!"

The bear tried to copy the little girl, but he stumbled and plopped down with his four paws in a tangle. "I know, you need some music!" said Apolline, running to her tape player, and the music of Camille Saint-Saëns' famous *Carnival of the Animals* filled the room.

When the bear heard the music, his clumsiness melted away and he began to soar around the room gracefully, carried away with delight. His paws, suddenly as light as feathers, barely touched the floor. His body stretched out and floated elegantly through the air like a shimmering, whirling soap bubble.

It was an incredible sight, magical. What an acrobat! He hopped . . . what charm!

Apolline giggled, laughed, tapped time with her toes, applauded each move. It was a triumph! When the bear took his final bow, she rushed over to him, grasped his big front paws in her little hands, and shook them firmly. Now he laughed too, gave Apolline a hug, and she almost disappeared into his thick fur.

"You were fantastic, Bear! Fantastic!" And the clumsy bear felt like he was dancing on air again.
Soon the two of them were dancing on air together.

As a flood rises in the
surrounding countryside, a
young boy sets about trying
to rescue the various creatures
that inhabit his garden with the
help of his toy ark, thereby creating
a fascinating floating world.

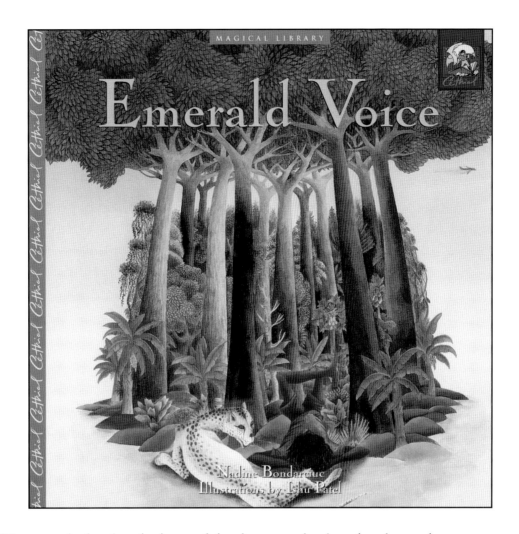

Bajho of the Kwayu tribe lived in the heart of the Amazuma land on the plains where once grew the mightiest rainforest in the world. His ancestors called it the Emerald Forest. Over the years the forest was destroyed. Only a group of twelve trees managed to survive.

These were the most precious trees in the world to Bajho and his tribe. Without them, the tribe could not survive. Though it was tiny, this forest provided them with shelter, medicine, and food. There were bananas, papayas,mangos, pineapples, avocados, cocoa, walnuts, cashew nuts, stilt palms, and rubber trees. The tribe extracted remedies from the eucalyptus and cinchona trees as well as from the surrounding herbs and plants. Bajho cherished each tree as he would a friend.

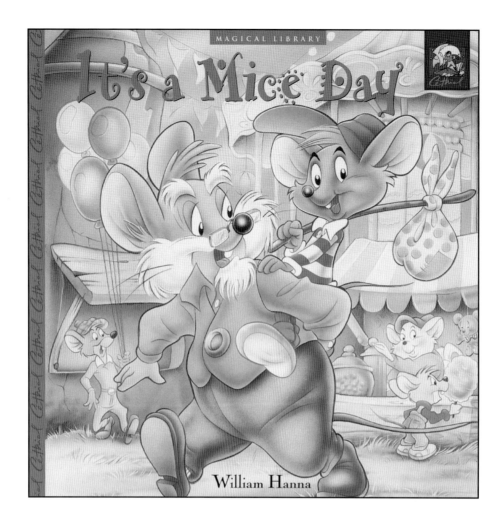

MAGICAL LIBRARY

It's a Mice Day

William Hanna

Little Bo pulled the covers up high
And tugged them close round his head.
There's no place that Little Bo rather would be
Than right in his soft featherbed.

One morning the Postman peeked into his room;
He knew he'd find Little Bo there.
The one mighty toot that he blew on his flute
Made Bo jump wide awake in the air.

Cêthial

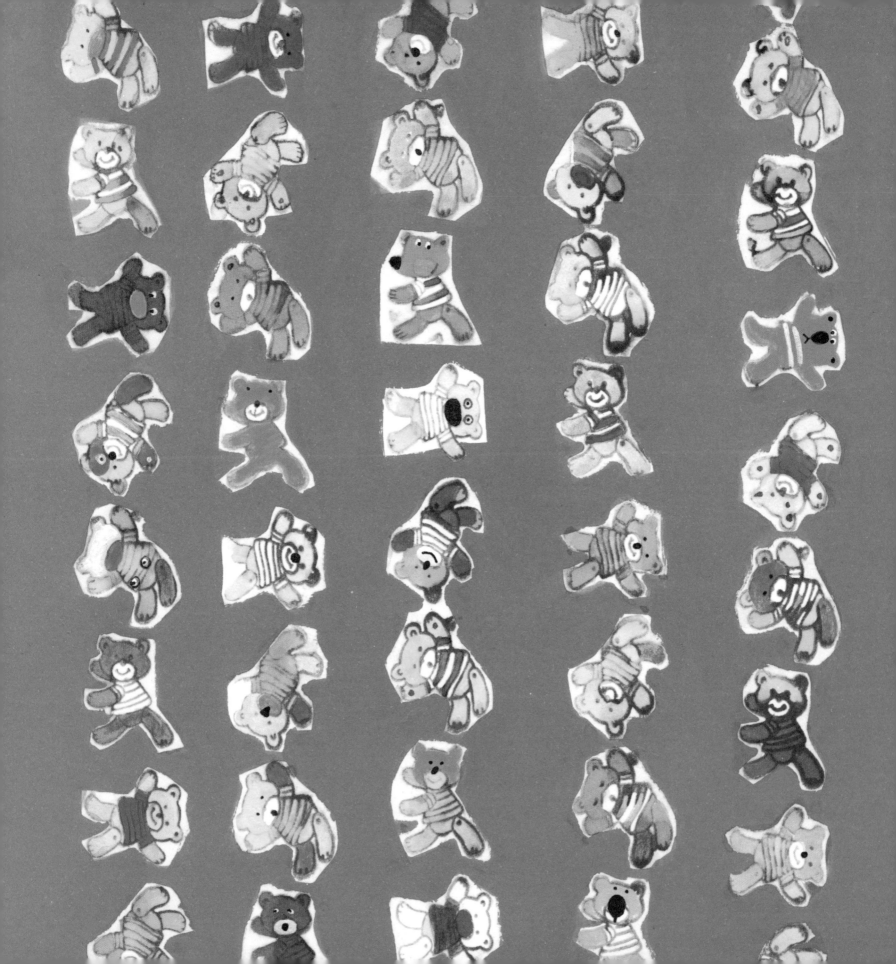